7455 W. CORNELIA AVE.
CHICAGO, IL 60634

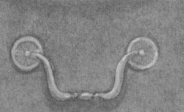

D1573202

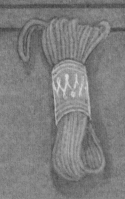

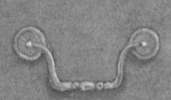

DUNNING BRANCH
7455 W. CORNELIA AVE.
CHICAGO, IL 60634

Marjorie Pickthall

The Worker
in Sandalwood

A Christmas Eve Miracle

illustrated by
Frances Tyrrell

Dutton Children's Books · New York

Acknowledgment

Thanks to the de Maio family and to
Madame and Monsieur le curé

Text adapted from a story by Marjorie Pickthall
Illustrations copyright © 1991 by Frances Tyrrell

All rights reserved. No part of this publication may be reproduced or
transmitted in any form or by any means, electronic or mechanical, including photocopy,
recording, or any information storage and retrieval system now known or to be invented,
without permission in writing from the publisher, except by a reviewer who
wishes to quote brief passages in connection with a review written for
inclusion in a magazine, newspaper, or broadcast.

CIP Data is available.

First published in the United States 1994 by
Dutton Children's Books,
a division of Penguin Books USA Inc.
375 Hudson Street, New York, New York 10014
Originally published in Toronto, Ontario, 1991 by
Lester Publishing Limited, Toronto.
Typography by Carolyn Boschi
Printed in Hong Kong
First American Edition
1 3 5 7 9 10 8 6 4 2
ISBN 0-525-45332-6

R01050 46670

CHICAGO PUBLIC LIBRARY
DUNNING BRANCH
7455 W. CORNELIA AVE.
CHICAGO, IL 60634

For Colin at Sunrise

I like to think of this as a true story, but you who read may please yourselves, siding either with the curé, who says Hyacinthe dreamed it all and did the carving himself in his sleep, or with Madame. I am sure that Hyacinthe thinks it true, and so does Madame, but then she has the cabinet, with the little birds and the lilies carved at the corners. Monsieur le curé shrugs his patient shoulders, but then he is tainted with the infidelities of cities, good man, having been three times to Montréal and once, in an electric car, to Sainte Anne. He and Madame still talk it over whenever they meet, though it happened so many years ago, and each leaves the other forever unconvinced. Meanwhile, the dust gathers in the infinite fine lines of the little birds' feathers, and softens the lily stamens where Madame's duster cannot go. The wood, aging, takes on a golden gleam as of immemorial sunsets: that pale red wood, heavy with the scent of the ancient East, the wood that Hyacinthe loved.

It was the only wood of that kind which had ever been seen in Terminaison. Pierre L'Oreillard brought it into the workshop one morning: a small, heavy bundle wrapped in sacking, and then in burlap, and then in fine soft cloths. He laid it on a pile of shavings, unwrapped it carefully, and a dim sweetness filled the dark shed and hung heavily in the thin winter sunbeams.

Pierre L'Oreillard rubbed the wood respectfully with his knobby fingers. "It is sandalwood," he explained to Hyacinthe, pride of knowledge making him expansive, "a most precious wood that grows in warm countries. Smell it. It is sweeter than cedar. It is to make a cabinet for the old Madame at the big house. Thy great hands shall smooth the wood, boy, and I—I, Pierre the cabinetmaker—shall render it beautiful." Then he went out, locking the door behind him.

When he was gone, Hyacinthe laid down his plane, blew on his stiff fingers, and shambled slowly over to the wood. He was a great clumsy boy of fourteen, dark faced, slow of speech, dull eyed, and uncared for. He was clumsy because it is impossible to move gracefully when you are growing very big and fast on quite insufficient food. He was dull eyed because all eyes met his unlovingly; uncared for, because none knew the beauty of his soul. But his heavy young hands could carve simple things, like flowers and birds and beasts, to perfection, as the curé pointed out. Simon has a tobacco jar, carved with pinecones and squirrels, and the curé has a pipe whose bowl is the bloom of a lady's slipper, that I have seen. But it is all very long ago.

Hyacinthe knew that the making of the cabinet would fall to him, as most of the other work did. He touched the strange, sweet wood, and at last laid his cheek against it, while the fragrance caught his breath. "How beautiful it is," said Hyacinthe, and for a moment his eyes glowed and he was happy. Then the light passed, and with bent head he shuffled back to his bench through a foam of white shavings curling almost to his knees.

M adame perhaps will want the cabinet next week, for that
is Christmas," said Hyacinthe, and he fell to work harder than ever,
though it was so cold in the shed that his breath hung like a little
silver cloud and the steel stung his hands. There was a tiny window
to his right, through which, when it was clear of frost, one looked
on Terminaison, and that was cheerful and made one whistle.
But to the left, through the chink of the ill-fitting door, there was

nothing but the forest and the road dying away in it, and the trees moving heavily under the snow. Yet from there came all Hyacinthe's silent dreams and reluctant fancies, which he sometimes found himself able to tell—in wood, not words.

Brandy was good at the Cinq Châteaux, and Pierre L'Oreillard gave Hyacinthe plenty of directions, but no further help with the cabinet.

That is to be finished for Madame on the festival, dullard," said he, cuffing Hyacinthe's ears furiously, "finished, with a prettiness about the corners, hearest thou, dolt? I suffer from a delicacy of the constitution and a little feebleness in the legs these days, so that I cannot handle the tools. I must leave this work to thee, clumsy. See it is done properly, and stand up and touch a hand to thy cap when I address thee, you great oaf."

"Yes, monsieur," said Hyacinthe wearily.

It is hard, when you do all the work, to be cuffed into the bargain, and fourteen is not very old. Hyacinthe went to work on the cabinet with slow, exquisite skill, but on the eve of Noël he was still at work, and the cabinet not completed. It meant a thrashing from Pierre if the morrow came and found it still unfinished, and Pierre's thrashings were cruel. But it was growing into a thing of perfection under Hyacinthe's slow hands, and he would not hurry over it.

"Then work on it all night, and show it to me all completed in the morning, or thy bones shall mourn thy idleness," said Pierre with a flicker of his little eyes. And he shut Hyacinthe into the workshop with a smoky lamp, his tools, and the sandalwood cabinet.

It was nothing unusual. The boy had often been left before to finish a piece of work overnight while Pierre went off to his brandies. But this was Christmas Eve, and Hyacinthe was very tired. The cold crept into the shed until even the scent of the sandalwood could not make him dream himself warm, and the roof cracked sullenly in the frost. There came upon Hyacinthe one of those awful, hopeless despairs that children know. "In all the world, nothing!" said he, staring at the dull flame. "No place, no heart, no love! O kind God, is there a place or love for me in another world?"

I cannot endure to think of Hyacinthe, poor lad, shut up despairing in the workshop with his loneliness, his cold, and his hunger, on the eve of Christmas. He looked at the chisel in his hand, and thought that by a touch of that he might be at peace, somewhere not far from God, only it was forbidden. Then came the tears, and great sobs that sickened and deafened him so that he scarcely heard the gentle rattling of the latch.

At least, I suppose it came then, but it may have been later. The story is all so vague here. I think that Hyacinthe must have gone to the door, opening it upon the still woods and the frosty stars, and the lad who stood outside must have said, "I see you are working late, friend. May I come in?" or something like it.

Hyacinthe brushed his ragged sleeve across his eyes and opened the door wider with a little nod to the other to enter. Those lonely villages strung along the great river see strange wayfarers adrift inland from the sea. Hyacinthe said to himself that surely here was such a one.

Afterward he told the curé that for a moment he had been bewildered. Blinking into the stranger's eyes, he lost for a flash the first impression of youth and received one of some incredible age or sadness. But this also passed and he knew that the wanderer's eyes were only quiet, very quiet. As he turned within the door, smiling at Hyacinthe and shaking some snow from his fur cap, he did not seem more than sixteen or so.

It is very cold outside," he said. "There is a big oak tree on the edge of the fields that has split in the frost and frightened all the little squirrels asleep there. Next year it will make an even better home for them. And see what I found close by!" He opened his fingers and showed Hyacinthe a little sparrow lying unruffled in his palm.

"Poor thing!" whispered Hyacinthe. "Poor thing. Is it dead then?" He touched it with a gentle forefinger.

"No," answered the strange boy, "it is not dead. We'll put it here among the shavings, not far from the lamp, and it will be well by morning."

He smiled at Hyacinthe again, and the shambling lad felt as if the scent of sandalwood had deepened, and the lamp flame burned clearer. But the stranger's eyes were only quiet, quiet.

"Have you come far?" asked Hyacinthe. "It is a bad season for traveling, and the wolves are out in the woods."

"A long way," said the other, "a long, long way. I heard a child cry...."

There is no child here," answered Hyacinthe, shaking his head. "Monsieur L'Oreillard is not fond of children. He says they cost too much money. But if you have come far, you must be cold and hungry, and I have no food or fire. At the Cinq Châteaux you will find both."

The stranger looked at him again with those quiet eyes, and Hyacinthe fancied his face was familiar. "I will stay here," he said. "You are very late at work and you are unhappy."

"Why, as to that," answered Hyacinthe, rubbing again at his cheeks and ashamed of his tears, "most of us are sad at one time or another, the good God knows. Stay here and welcome if it pleases you, and you may take a share of my bed, though it is no more than a pile of balsam boughs and an old blanket, in the loft. But I must work at this cabinet, for the drawers must be finished and the handles put on and these corners carved, all by the holy morning, or my wages will be paid with a stick."

You have a hard master," put in the other boy, "if he would pay you with blows upon the feast of Noël."

"He is hard enough," said Hyacinthe, "but once he gave me a dinner of sausages and white wine, and one summer, some melons. If my eyes will stay open, I will finish this by morning, but indeed I am sleepy. Stay with me an hour or so, friend, and talk to me of your wanderings so that the time may pass more quickly."

"I will tell you of the country where I was a child," answered the stranger.

And while Hyacinthe worked, he told of sunshine and dust; of the shadows of vine leaves on the flat white walls of a house; of rosy doves on the flat roof; of the flowers that come in the spring, crimson and blue, and the white cyclamen in the shadow of the rocks; of the olive, the myrtle, and the almond; until Hyacinthe's slow fingers ceased working and his sleepy eyes blinked wonderingly.

"See what you have done, friend," he said at last. "You have told of such pretty things that I have done no work for an hour. And now the cabinet will never be finished and I shall get a beating."

"Let me help you," smiled the other. "I also was raised a carpenter."

At first Hyacinthe would not, fearing to trust the sweet wood out of his own hands, but at length he allowed the stranger to fit in one of the little drawers, and so deftly was the work done that Hyacinthe pounded his fists on the bench in admiration. "You have a pretty knack," he cried. "It seemed as if you did but hold the drawer in your hands a moment, and hey! ho! it jumped into its place!"

"Let me fit in the other little drawers, while you rest a while," said the wanderer. So Hyacinthe curled up among the shavings, and the stranger fell to work upon the little cabinet of sandalwood.

Here begins what the curé believes is a dream within a dream. Sometimes I am forced to agree with him, but then I see as clearly as with old Madame's eyes, and with her and Hyacinthe, I say, "I believe."

Hyacinthe said that he lay upon the shavings in the sweetness of the sandalwood, and was very tired. He thought of the country where the stranger had been a boy; of the flowers on the hills; of the laughing leaves of aspen and poplar; of the golden flowering anise and the golden sun upon the dusty roads; until he was warm. All the time, through these pictures, as through a painted veil, he was aware of that other boy with quiet eyes, at work upon the cabinet, smoothing, fitting, polishing. "He does better work than I," thought Hyacinthe, but he was not jealous. And again he thought, "It is growing toward morning. In a little while I will get up and help him." But he did not, for the dream of warmth and the smell of the sandalwood held him in a sweet drowse. Also, he said that he thought the stranger was singing as he worked, for there seemed to be a sense of some music in the shed, though he could not tell whether it came from the other boy's lips or from the shabby, old tools as he used them. "The stars are much paler," thought Hyacinthe, "and soon it will be morning and the corners are not carved yet. I must get up and help this kind one in a little moment. Only I am so tired, and the music and the sweetness seem to wrap me and fold me close, so that I may not move."

He lay without moving, and behind the forest there shone
a pale glow of some indescribable color that was neither green nor
blue, while in Terminaison the church bells began to ring. "Day will
soon be here!" thought Hyacinthe, immovable in that deep dream
of his, "and with day will come Monsieur L'Oreillard and his stick.
I must get up and help, for even yet the corners are not carved."

But he did not get up. Instead, he saw the stranger look at
him again, then lay a brown finger lightly upon the four empty

corners of the cabinet. And Hyacinthe saw the reddish wood ripple
and heave and break, as little clouds when the wind goes through
the sky. And out of them thrust forth little birds, and after them
the lilies for a moment living, but even while Hyacinthe looked,
growing hard and reddish brown and settling back into the sweet
wood. Then the stranger laid all the tools neatly in order and, opening the door quietly, went away into the woods.

Hyacinthe lay still among the shavings for a long time, and then he crept slowly to the door. The sun, not yet risen, set its first beams upon the delicate mist of frost afloat beneath the trees, and so all the world was aflame with splendid gold. Far away down the road a dim figure seemed to move amid the glory, but the splendor was such that Hyacinthe was blinded. His breath came sharply as the glow beat in great waves on the wretched shed, on the foam of shavings, on the cabinet with the little birds, and the lilies carved at the corners.

"Blessed be the Lord," whispered Hyacinthe, clasping his slow hands. And the little sparrow came from his nest among the shavings and shook his wings to the light.